Captain Jack
and the
Pirates

For Theo, Tara and Rosie – P.B.

For Anna Collette – H.O.

PUFFIN BOOKS
UK | USA | Canada | Ireland | Australia | India | New Zealand | South Africa
Puffin Books is part of the Penguin Random House group of companies
whose addresses can be found at global.penguinrandomhouse.com.
First published 2015
This edition published 2016
Text copyright © Peter Bently, 2015
Illustrations copyright © Helen Oxenbury, 2015
The moral right of the author and illustrator has been asserted
A CIP catalogue record for this book is available from the British Library
Printed in China   001
978–0–723–26929–8

Captain Jack
and the
Pirates

PETER BENTLY ★ HELEN OXENBURY

PUFFIN

Jack, Zak and Caspar,
brave mariners three,
were building a galleon down by the sea.

And there stood the galleon, fit for the fray,
as brave Captain Jack ordered,
"Anchors aweigh!"

A shirt
and a bib,
an inflatable ring . . .

For cannons three buckets were
just the right thing.

A stick for the mainmast
and one for the yard . . .

Tying the two sticks together was hard.

Up rose the sides
and the stern and the bow.
Zak, the ship's bosun, worked hard
on the prow.

They hoisted the mainsail,
    the flag was unfurled,
and Jack and his pirates set off round the world.

    Through oceans unknown,
        many miles from the land,
    sailed swashbuckling Jack and his buccaneer band.

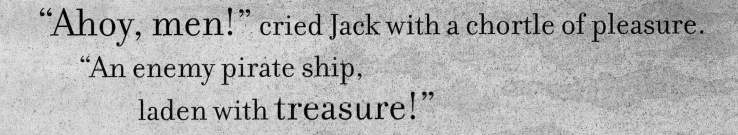

"Ahoy, men!" cried Jack with a chortle of pleasure.
"An enemy pirate ship,
laden with treasure!"

"Steer a course after them, good Bosun Zak!"
And Zak answered brightly,
"Aye, aye, Captain Jack!"

"Caspar, take care of the cannons!" Jack said.
"Look sharp in the crow's nest, Cabin Boy Ted!"

As they closed in, every man did his duty,
hungry for glory and enemy booty.

Their proud pirate flag
            fluttered high in the breeze —
and then the ships sailed
            into **stormier** seas . . .

The wind became stronger.
            "Hold on to the sail!"
cried Jack as they battled a **tropical gale.**

Down came the rain
as the **hurricane** roared.
Down came the sail,
and then . . .

. . . man overboard!

The sides of the galleon started to slip.
"Quick!" cried the captain.
"Abandon the ship!"

Jack and his shipmates all struggled ashore.
"We're **marooned** on an island," he cried.
"Let's explore!"

"Those enemy pirates
were shipwrecked here too.
Let's hunt for their treasure!"
said Jack to his crew.

"Caspar, stay here while
we see what we find."
Said Zak, "Just in case
we're attacked from behind."

The captain and bosun spied out the view.
And then a loud voice cried out —

"Jack,
is that you?"

"The enemy pirates!"
hissed Jack to his mate.
"We must rescue Caspar
before it's too late!"

They ran down the hill
    and Jack cried, "Oho!
Brave little Caspar
    has seen off the foe!"

"And, look, here's their hideout!"
    Jack hollered with joy.
"The pirates have fled, lads,
        and . . ."

" . . . treasure ahoy!"

Jack and his shipmates
all gasped in delight
as they hungrily stared
at the glorious sight.

"Right, let's divide up our booty," said Jack.

"Caught you!" a voice cried.

The pirates
were
back!

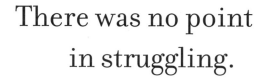
There was no point
in struggling.

Their hopes were all wrecked.

Jack sighed,
"Now we'll all walk the plank,
I expect."

But those pirates were friendly.
They shared out their treasure —

and added **three** ice creams . . .

. . . just for good measure!